BEACH DAY

Library of Congress Control Number: 2023902780
ISBN: 978-1-7375544-1-7
Character Design by Anja Jaeger
Story Design by The Purple Door Publishing House

To Siouxsie,
who got me through it.

BEACH DAY

A lil' Boo Adventure

By Anja Jaeger

A Note from the Author

Throughout my life I have visited many beaches all over the world and no matter what, the day never goes exactly as planned. Things move differently where water meets land. The beach has its own kinds of sounds and its own rhythm. It's easy to get lost in what you're doing and find things you weren't looking for. The best way to enjoy a day at the beach is by staying in the moment and moving on to each new experience as it comes.
And it's even better with a friend.

Made in the USA
Monee, IL
29 April 2023

32480897R00031